ELMER AND THE DRAGON

ELMER AND THE DRAGON

STORY BY
RUTH STILES GANNETT

ILLUSTRATIONS BY
RUTH CHRISMAN GANNETT

RANDOM HOUSE · NEW YORK

2 266

For MICHAEL
and PETER

CONTENTS

Chapter One

TANGERINA

Into the evening sky flew Elmer Elevator aboard the gentle baby dragon, leaving Wild Island behind forever. Elmer, who was nine years old, had just rescued the dragon from the ferocious animals who lived on the island. An old alley cat told him how the dragon had been hurt when he fell from a cloud onto the island, and how the wild animals had made him their miserable prisoner. Elmer, feeling sorry for the dragon, and also hoping to fly on his back, had set off to the rescue.

Now the dragon was free, and happy and grateful, and he said, "Elmer, you were wonderful to come all the way to Wild Island just to rescue me. I'll never be

9

able to thank you enough!"

"Oh, that's all right," said Elmer. "Flying on your back makes all my trouble worth while."

"Then I'll take you on a trip! Where would you like to go?"

"Everywhere," said Elmer. "The trouble is that I ran away ten days ago to rescue you, and I guess I ought to be getting home."

"Well, at least I can fly you there."

"That would be swell," said Elmer, peering over the dragon's side. "Let's rest tonight down there on Tangerina Island, and start the trip tomorrow."

"Fine," said the dragon, swooping down and landing beneath a tree on the beach of Tangerina.

Elmer slid down and took off his knapsack. "You're beautiful!" he said, admiring the dragon's blue and yellow stripes, his red horn and eyes, his great long tail and especially his gold-colored wings shining in the faint moonlight.

"It's very kind of you to say so," said the dragon, suddenly feeling very hungry. "What's there to eat around here?"

"Tangerines all over the place!" said Elmer, picking one and peeling it for the dragon.

"Pew! Pew! What a terrible taste!" choked the dragon, spitting out the tangerine as hard as he could.

"What do dragons eat?" asked Elmer.

"I used to enjoy the skunk cabbages and the ostrich ferns on Wild Island, but I don't see any here," said the dragon, looking anxiously up and down the empty beach.

"Maybe you'd like the tangerine peelings?" suggested Elmer.

The dragon closed his eyes and carefully bit off a small corner of a piece of a peel. Then he jumped up yelling, "Why, they're delicious!"

So, Elmer and the dragon ate nineteen tangerines, Elmer the insides and the dragon the peels. A chilly wind blew along the beach and the dragon curled his great long tail around the boy to keep him warm. "Good night!" said Elmer, resting his head on his knapsack. "I can't wait for the trip home tomorrow."

Next morning, as the sun edged over the horizon, the dragon rubbed his eyes, stretched his wings and yawned. "My, but it's good to be free again! By the way, Elmer, where do you live?"

"In Nevergreen City near Evergreen Park on the coast of Popsicornia," mumbled Elmer, who was already awake and eating tangerines.

"I hope you know how to get there," said the dragon.

"Don't you?" asked Elmer.

"No, don't you?" asked the dragon.

"No," said Elmer. "You see, I came here in the bottom of a boat and I couldn't see where I was going."

"The seagulls will know," said the dragon. "They

follow ships out to sea."

"I'll go ask one," said Elmer, suddenly remembering that it would be nice to be home for his father's birthday. He walked down to the water where a very old gull was blinking at the morning sun.

"Excuse me," said Elmer, "but did you ever hear of Nevergreen City?"

"Of course," croaked the very old gull. "I lived there before I followed a ship to Tangerina, but I wouldn't dream of going back now."

"That's very interesting," said Elmer, "but would you know how to go if you did want to?"

"Certainly!" answered the old gull, pointing his right wing toward the ocean. "Just fly in exactly that direction until you get there."

Elmer took out his compass and found that this direction was West North West. "Is it very far?"

"Far? I should say so!"

"Well, thanks a lot," said Elmer.

"I'm kind of worried," said the dragon. "Suppose we never find it?"

"We'll find it, all right," said Elmer, who was a tiny bit worried himself.

The dragon ran along the beach warming up his wings while Elmer packed sixty-nine tangerines, as many as his knapsack would hold. Besides the tangerines, he had in his knapsack all sorts of things left over from the rescue, including seven pink lollipops (which he was saving for an emergency), half a pack-

age of rubber bands, three sticks of chewing gum, a
very good jackknife, and a burlap bag. Of course, he
kept his compass in his pocket where it would be
handy, and he wore his black rubber boots.

"Are you ready?" asked Elmer.

"Jump on!" said the dragon.

Elmer clambered onto the dragon's back and took
one last look at Tangerina and the blue and white
waves skipping in from the cold ocean onto the sandy
beach.

Chapter Two

STORM

They flew all morning, high above the endless blue and white waves. Elmer sat feeling the wind on his face, listening to the whir of the dragon's wings, and watching the compass to make sure they were going in the right direction.

"I see a rock down there," said the dragon in the late afternoon. "Let's rest a bit."

"Good idea," said Elmer.

The dragon circled down to the rock, landing on all four feet. Elmer unpacked eleven tangerines and as he and the dragon ate they watched the sky turn from blue to gray and then to dark gray.

"Looks like a storm," said Elmer.

"Yes," said the dragon. "Do you think we'd better wait here or go on?"

"If the wind's bad, the waves will wash right over this rock," said Elmer. "But if we keep going maybe we can fly away from the storm."

"Let's hurry on," said the dragon, and up they flew while the waves grew whiter and wilder.

"I felt a drop of rain," said Elmer, looking up at the blackening sky.

Suddenly a ferocious wind rushed up from behind, pushing them forward faster and faster. Thunder crackled all around them, and cold hard rain beat down upon them.

"I wish I had my raincoat," yelled Elmer.

"I wish it weren't raining!" panted the dragon. "My wings are getting heavy and I can't fly very well. Besides, I hate thunder!"

The wind blew harder and the rain was colder. Elmer looked at his compass and cried through the

rumbling storm, "We're going in the wrong direction!"

"I can't help it. The wind's too strong. I can't fight against it," screamed the dragon.

Elmer put away his compass and looked down at the thrashing spray. He could hear the dragon breathing hard, and he watched his wings beating slower and slower. He wondered how long the tired dragon could fly through the crashing storm.

"I can't go on," puffed the dragon, and he sank through the rain nearer to the cold wild water. Elmer shut his eyes and held on as hard as he could, trying not to cry or think about home.

"I'm sorry," huffed the dragon, "that I couldn't keep my promise."

"Oh, that's all right. You did your best," sobbed Elmer.

And then the dragon sank lower, closer to the water.

Splash!

"Elmer, we're safe! I landed on sand!" yelled the dragon. "But don't get off, because the water is up to my knees."

Elmer opened his eyes and looked around, but it was too dark to see anything. "Are you very uncomfortable?" he screamed above the noise of the storm.

"It's not too bad," shrieked the dragon, "but I think

the water's getting deeper."

"Gosh, maybe you're sinking in quicksand!"

"No, I don't think so. Anyway, where else can I go? We'll just have to wait here. Why don't you take a nap? I can sleep standing up, you know."

"A nap in the middle of the ocean in the middle of a storm?"

"Why not? There's nothing else to do."

So, Elmer lay down along the dragon's back and they both were so tired that they fell asleep while the thunder boomed all around them.

"Elmer! Elmer! My stomach's under water," cried the dragon, suddenly waking up an hour later.

Elmer looked around. The storm was nearly over, but all he could see was drizzly rain and the water lapping against the dragon's stomach. "Poor dragon, would you like a pink lollipop?" asked Elmer, deciding that this was a real emergency.

"I'd rather have a cup of hot milkweed milk, but I

guess a lollipop would help," said the dragon.

Elmer unpacked one for himself and one for the dragon, and then carefully crawled along the dragon's neck until he could put the lollipop into his mouth.

"It does help a little," shivered the dragon.

As they were sucking their pink lollipops in the middle of the ocean the drizzly rain turned into thick, thick fog and then the water began to get shallower.

"My stomach's out of water again," announced the dragon cheerfully.

"I know why the water goes up and down!" exclaimed Elmer. "It's the tide, and we're on a sand bar near some land, and just as soon as the fog lifts we'll be able to see what kind of land it is!"

"I hope it's dry land," said the dragon.

All night the water got shallower and shallower, and Elmer and the dragon were too excited to sleep. Finally, as the sun rose, even the dragon's feet were out of water, and the fog began to rise.

Chapter Three

THE SAND BAR

The fog rolled along the sand bar and out over the water and suddenly Elmer shouted, "There, behind you! Look at the pretty little green island!"

"But Elmer, I can't! I can't move. Oh, Elmer, I hurt all over." The dragon grunted and groaned and strained and struggled but he was too stiff to move at all. "Elmer, do you really see dry land, not far off?"

"Nice near dry green land, and the water's shallow all the way. Are you sure you can't move?"

"I'll try again. How stupid! I can't even see the land after waiting here for it all night long in the soaking wet water," complained the dragon, glaring at the miles of ocean before him, which was all he could see.

Elmer walked around to the dragon's head and pretended not to notice that he was crying.

"Elmer, I guess I'm not much of a dragon. A little storm comes along and forces me down, and I stand in a little water for a little while and it makes me so stiff that I can't move a single muscle."

"That's not at all true," said Elmer. "It was a big storm, and you stood in a lot of cold water for a very long time, and besides, you're only a baby dragon and you're not used to flying long distances. And just as soon as the sun dries you off, you'll be unstiff again. Have another lollipop."

"Thanks, Elmer."

"But you'd better get unstiff pretty quick because the tide will come in and you'll be up to your stomach in water again."

"No, no," whimpered the dragon.

"Well, I'll hang on your neck and see if it will bend," suggested Elmer. He jumped up and caught

the dragon's neck. He dangled for a moment and then
both he and the neck thumped down on the sand.

"Ouch!" groaned Elmer and the dragon.

"Now, can you see the island between your legs?"

The dragon carefully curled his head under to look,
and then he shouted, "I see it now, Elmer! It's really
there. What a lovely little dry island! Now help me
limber up my right front leg."

Elmer pulled very hard on the dragon's right front
leg until it would bend. Then he worked on the left

back leg, and the left front leg, and the right back leg, and started all over again with the right front leg. At last the dragon could turn around and walk. By now it was hot, and steam rose up all along the dragon's back as the sun beat down on his water-soaked wings.

Elmer started for the island and the dragon hobbled slowly behind. They went along the sand bar as far as they could and then waded into the shallow water. Elmer was still wearing his black rubber boots, but the dragon muttered, "I hate oceans!" as he splashed along stiff-leggedly.

Finally they came to the pebbly beach of the tiny island. Above them rose a cliff and green vines hung over the edge, making a pool of shade. Elmer and the dragon sat down and ate fifteen tangerines, leaving forty-three more in the knapsack. "I wonder who lives on this island," said Elmer, wiping his mouth on his sleeve. "I think that's a path over there. Come on, let's go exploring."

"I'm afraid I'll have to rest a while longer," said the dragon. "My wings are still wet and heavy, and I'm awfully hungry. Tangerine peels don't really fill me up, and I'm terribly thirsty, and maybe I'm going to faint."

"Then you rest here in the shade while I go to look for food and water," said Elmer, as he picked up his knapsack and went off to follow the little path.

Chapter Four

THE ISLAND

The path wound between boulders on the beach and then rose steeply through a crack in the cliff. Elmer scrambled up, bracing himself between the rock walls until he could find the next toe-hole. Just as he thought he could go no farther he found an old log ladder going straight up to the top of the cliff. "Somebody must live here," he thought as he climbed up the last rung and sat down. All around him rose beautiful tall pine trees standing in rows, and he said, "Trees don't grow in rows all by themselves. These pines were planted here by somebody a long time ago."

Elmer ate four more tangerines, and then started through the pines to look for food and water. At last he came out onto a sloping meadow. He saw a brook winding its way down the slope and he ran to take a long cool drink.

"The dragon will be happy to see this," he thought. "But I do wish I'd find somebody to tell us where we are and how to get home." He followed the brook up the slope into an old, old apple orchard. Some of the trees had rotted down to stumps, but they had been planted in rows, too. Elmer didn't see anybody anywhere, so he followed the brook back down the slope to a place where it made a pool of clear, cold water. He stooped down for another drink and found an old wooden bucket carved out of the trunk of a tree. "This bucket hasn't been used for many years," he thought as he scraped off the moss and weeds. "Maybe nobody lives here any more."

Elmer left the bucket beside the pool and followed the brook through ferns and bushes until it turned into a swamp. "Skunk cabbages and ostrich ferns all over the place!" yelled Elmer, who was worried about the hungry, thirsty baby dragon. He quickly pulled up six skunk cabbages and ran back through the bushes to the pool. He dipped the bucket half full, threw in the cabbages, and hurried through the meadow to the pines and the dragon.

He knew he couldn't go down the ladder with the bucket, so he crawled to the edge of the cliff and peered through the vines. There was the wilted baby dragon, snoring in the shade.

"Dragon! Dragon! Wake up! I've got water and skunk cabbages for you!"

The dragon slowly opened one eye and looked up at Elmer. Then he quickly opened the other and said, "Where?"

"Right here in a bucket. But I can't bring it down to you. You'll have to let me pour the water down your throat. Ready?"

"Ready," said the dragon, tipping back his head.

Elmer aimed and poured and the dragon drank. Then Elmer threw down the cabbages one by one, and the dragon caught each cabbage in the air, laughing and crying at the same time because he was so happy and hungry and thirsty.

"That's all," said Elmer, "but there's lots more up on the island, and ostrich ferns, too. Can you fly up now?"

"Ostrich ferns! I'd better be able to fly," said the dragon, stiffly flapping his gold-colored wings. He hobbled along the beach, gave a little jump, and fluttered up to the top of the cliff. "I'm not the dragon I used to be," he panted, "but I'll get you home yet, Elmer. Don't you worry about that."

"Oh, I know you will. I'm not the least bit worried," said Elmer, although he had secretly hoped to find people on the island, and a boat going home, and all sorts of good things to eat.

Chapter Five

FLUTE, THE CANARY

Elmer and the dragon rested awhile on top of the cliff, watching the waves spreading out over the sand bar. Suddenly a little voice chirped, "You're Elmer Elevator, aren't you?"

Elmer was too startled to answer.

"Aren't you? Of course, it has been three years, and people do change."

Elmer looked all around but he couldn't see anybody. "Yes, I'm Elmer, but who and where are you?" he asked.

"Look up in the tree above you. It's me, Flute."

Elmer and the dragon looked up and there he was, Flute the canary—funny little Flute with two black

eyebrows and one black feather in each wing.

"Oh, Flute! How glad I am to see you. But how did you get here?"

"I flew here the day you let me out of my cage when your mother went to answer the doorbell. This is where all the escaped canaries live—Feather Island, we call it. But what on earth are you doing here?"

"Well, I just rescued this baby dragon, and he was flying me home, only we got caught in a storm and landed here instead. And now he's got to rest and get plenty of food and water before we can go on."

"Does he eat canaries?"

"I should say not!" snorted the dragon. "Only fruits and vegetables and lollipops."

"That's a relief," said Flute. "I almost didn't talk to you because the rest of the canaries were afraid. I'll just tell them everything's all right," and Flute trilled loudly in every direction. Soon, canaries were chirping all over the island, and the pine trees rustled with fluttering wings.

"Let's go eat," said the dragon, who was bored and still hungry and thirsty. So Flute flew down and rode on Elmer's shoulder as they walked through the pines.

"Tell me, Flute, do people live on this island?" asked Elmer.

"No. Just canaries."

"That's what I thought. Well, how have you been getting along without my mother? She's never stopped worrying about you."

"Quite well, thank you," said Flute, "but I'm beginning to suffer from the island disease."

"What's that?"

"I know it sounds silly, but the whole island is sick with curiosity, and old King Can is actually dying of it."

"Who's King Can?" asked the dragon, becoming somewhat interested.

"He's the king of the canaries. He's really King

Can XI. His ancestors, King and Queen Can I, were the first canaries to live on the island. They came with a party of settlers. But the settlers sailed away after a month or two, and they left King Can and his wife behind."

"Now I understand about the ladder and the bucket and pine trees and the apple orchard," said Elmer.

"Yes," said Flute, "they are the work of the settlers. But to continue: Migrating birds often stop by here and King Can, being lonesome, told them to ask escaped canaries to live on his island. But even after many canaries had come, he was never well or happy. And when the other birds asked 'Why not?' King Can would answer, 'I'm dying of curiosity.' Pretty soon, the other canaries grew curious to know why he was so curious, but he told the reason only to his eldest son. And so they all grew sick with curiosity. Finally, when King Can I was a very old canary, he did die of curiosity and his eldest son became King Can II."

"Skunk cabbage! I smell skunk cabbage," interrupted the dragon right in the middle of the story, because by this time they had come out onto the meadow.

"It's right over there in the swamp," said Elmer, and the dragon lumbered off to eat and to drink cold water.

"King Can II, III, IV, V, VI, VII, VIII, IX and X all died of curiosity as very old canaries, and now King Can XI is sick with it. And the rest of us are sick, too. I tell you, it's an awful thing," continued Flute.

"I suppose so," said Elmer. "I wonder what they could have been so curious about."

"See, there you go getting curious! What a great day it will be when this island gets over the plague of curiosity!"

"Maybe I could help King Can XI," suggested Elmer. "If *he* weren't curious any more, then nobody else would be curious to know *why* he's curious, and everybody would get well."

"That's right," said Flute. "Let's go see the King. He lives in the biggest tree in the forest."

Elmer yelled to the dragon that he'd be back soon, but all he could hear was loud munching and drinking noises in the bushes.

Chapter Six

KING CAN XI

Flute perched on Elmer's shoulder and together they went to the biggest tree in the forest. Flute flew up into the branches and Elmer heard him chirp, "Good morning, Queen Can. An old friend of mine has just arrived on the island, and I'd like to introduce him to the King."

"Is that your friend down there?" asked the sleek tiny Queen suspiciously.

"Yes. He let me out of my cage back in Nevergreen City."

"The King isn't feeling well, you know."

"I know, that's why I want to introduce my friend. I think he can help the King, perhaps."

"Well, I'll go see if he's receiving visitors. You wait here."

Soon the Queen flew back all flustered. "The King will be down right away. I was really surprised. He's never before been so eager to see anyone!"

Elmer felt flattered, and quickly tucked in his shirt and straightened his cap.

Suddenly the King flew out of the branches and landed at Elmer's feet. Elmer was disappointed. The King looked just like a canary, only bigger and fluffier than the others.

"This is my dear friend Elmer Elevator," said Flute.

"Hello. Won't you sit down?" said King Can XI.
"Thank you," said Elmer, squatting down on the
pine needles.

"It's a great honor to have you on our island," said the King.

"It's a great honor to be here," said Elmer.

"The Queen said that Flute said that you might be able to help me. Is that right?" asked the King.

"Yes," said Elmer. "I thought perhaps I could help you to find out whatever you're so curious to know, and then all the other birds wouldn't be curious to know *why* you're curious, and everybody would get well."

"Hmm," said the King. "Did you have some special plan?"

"You'd have to help by telling me what's bothering you," said Elmer.

"That's what I was afraid of! Why, this has been a family secret ever since my great–great–great–great–great–great–great–grandfather was a young canary. No, I couldn't possibly tell you!" snorted King Can XI.

"Then I can't help you after all," said Elmer, getting up. "I'm sorry I bothered Your Majesty about it. Good-by."

Elmer and Flute sadly started back through the pines.

"Ah, just a moment," called the King. "Maybe we could work out something. I'm awfully tired of being curious. Yes, by gosh, I believe I *will* tell you. But don't you dare tell anyone else!"

"I promise," said Elmer.

"Flute, go up and chatter with the Queen. Your friend and I wish to be alone."

The King whispered to Elmer, "You can't imagine how hard it is for me to tell you our family secret."

"I'm sure it's extremely difficult," said Elmer helpfully.

"Well, the secret is—the secret is—the secret is—oh, I can't tell you now. Could you come back at sundown? I just can't say it in the bright sunlight."

"I understand," said Elmer, "and I'll be glad to come back later." He called to Flute, who had been trying hard not to yawn in front of the Queen, and together they went to find the dragon.

"Well, did you see the King?" asked the dragon, who was resting comfortably beside the pool, his stomach bulging with skunk cabbages and ostrich ferns.

"Yes, but now I'm really curious. I'm to go back at sundown and then he's going to tell me the secret. It's a very old family secret."

"I just can't stand it! I can't stand it!" said Flute. "Oh, I'll be so glad to be rid of the curiosity plague."

"I'll do my best," said Elmer, taking a long drink of water and settling down beside the dragon to eat eight tangerines.

Elmer and the dragon fell fast asleep while Flute went all over the island spreading the news and waiting for sundown.

Chapter Seven

THE SECRET

"Wake up! Wake up! It's time to see the King!" chirped Flute as the red sun settled over the meadow. Elmer opened his eyes and forgot for a moment where he was. Then he jumped up and put on his knapsack.

"I want to come, too," yawned the dragon.

"You weren't invited," said Flute.

"Neither were you, Flute, come to think of it," said Elmer.

"Let's all go and see what happens," suggested the

dragon. So off they went to see the King. He was waiting for them at the foot of the very tall tree, nervously hopping from one foot to the other, pecking at imaginary mosquitoes.

"What's that?" he asked, pointing to the dragon.

"That's my good friend the baby dragon. I rescued him two days ago and now he's taking me home."

"I don't like him," said the King, feeling small and helpless.

"Oh, yes you do!" said Flute.

"Quiet, Flute! I guess I know what I like and what I don't!"

The dragon drooped his head and began to back away.

"Oh well," said the King, "come on back. If I'm going to tell the secret to anyone it'll never be a secret any more, and I suppose you might as well know, too. I do wish it weren't such an old secret."

Flute, the dragon and Elmer waited quietly while

the King looked at the ground, then up at the tree, and then down at the ground.

"Treasure!" he whispered so suddenly that they all jumped into the air. "At least I think it's treasure, but I can't find out without your help."

"Where?" asked Elmer.

"It's—it's—it's not very far from here," said the King. Elmer, Flute and the dragon looked every-which-way to see where the treasure could be.

"Oh gosh, I guess I'll have to tell you where, too," said poor old King Can XI. "It's buried—it's buried right under this tree—in a big iron chest."

"What sort of treasure?" asked Elmer.

"That's what I'm dying of curiosity to know," said the King.

"So that's it!" sighed Flute.

"And you're sure this is the right tree?" asked Elmer.

"Absolutely! You see, it's much bigger than the

others, and that's because it was the only one here when the settlers came. They planted the other pines and the apple orchard so they'd have wood and food when they returned. But they never came back, and their chest is still buried right here."

Everybody waited for the King to continue, but he didn't, so Elmer said, "Let's dig it up!"

"Yes, let's!" echoed Flute.

"All right," said the King. "My secret's all spoiled now, anyway. You'll find the shovel—under that rock."

"What shovel?" asked Elmer.

"The settlers left a shovel over there. It's rusty by now, but it's probably better than nothing."

Elmer went to get the shovel while the King danced around on the pine needles chirping, "I'm feeling better already." The Queen kept tittering and muttering to herself, "I never thought I'd live to see this day."

"Now, where should I begin digging?" asked Elmer.

"It's a rhyme," said the King. "It goes like this:
Four shovel lengths from the trunk of the pine,
Making the rock the guide for the line."
Elmer carefully measured the distance and began
to dig. The dragon did his best to help while Flute
and the King and Queen sat watching the hole grow-
ing deeper. By now it was dark in the pine forest, but
enough moonlight filtered through the branches of the
tall trees so that they could just see what they were
doing. They dug for six hours, without ever hitting a
root or a rock or anything like an iron chest.

"Are you certain this is the right place?" asked
Elmer, tired and discouraged.

"I'm positive!" said the King. Just then the moon
went under the clouds and Elmer's shovel hit something with a loud clang.

"The chest!" they all shouted, but it was too dark
to see. And they waited so long for the moon to come
out that they all went to sleep still waiting.

Chapter Eight

TREASURE

Flute woke up and trilled so loudly that he startled the King and the Queen and Elmer and the dragon wide awake. The other canaries had been up for an hour and were crowding around to see what was happening under the tree. Everybody peered into the big hole and gasped, "A real treasure chest, with a ring in the top! But how will we ever get it out?"

The King looked at Elmer, and Elmer looked at the dragon. "Dragon, do you think you could put your tail through the ring and pull up the chest?"

"I'll try," said the dragon, puffing up with importance as the swarms of canaries moved aside for him. He backed up to the hole, stuck his tail down and through the ring, and pulled.

Nothing happened.

"Couldn't you pull harder?" suggested the King.

"That's exactly what I was going to try. Just let me catch my breath," said the dragon somewhat crossly. "After all, I'm not used to lifting heavy chests with my tail." He took a deep, deep breath and pulled very, very hard, and suddenly the chest moved. He grunted and strained and struggled and panted and slowly, slowly hoisted the chest up out of the hole.

"Far enough!" yelled Elmer. "Now walk forward

and set it down."

Crash! The chest fell down on the pine needles and the dragon staggered off to sit down while the canaries shouted "Bravo!"

"Quiet! Quiet!" yelled King Can XI. "I am now about to tell you the last part of the secret. The key to this chest—the key to this chest—well, anyway, this is the last part of the secret. My illustrious ancestor, King Can I, stole the key from the settlers, and the key to this chest is in my nest. Go get it, Flute. No, never mind. I'll go get it myself."

The King flew up to his nest and down again with a big brass key in his beak. Elmer pried out the dirt in the keyhole with his jackknife and put in the key.

Click! The lock turned. Elmer threw back the lid, and picked up a note lying on top of a piece of heavy canvas. "Can you read what it says?" asked the King.

"Yes," said Elmer, feeling sick with excitement as he read the note aloud:

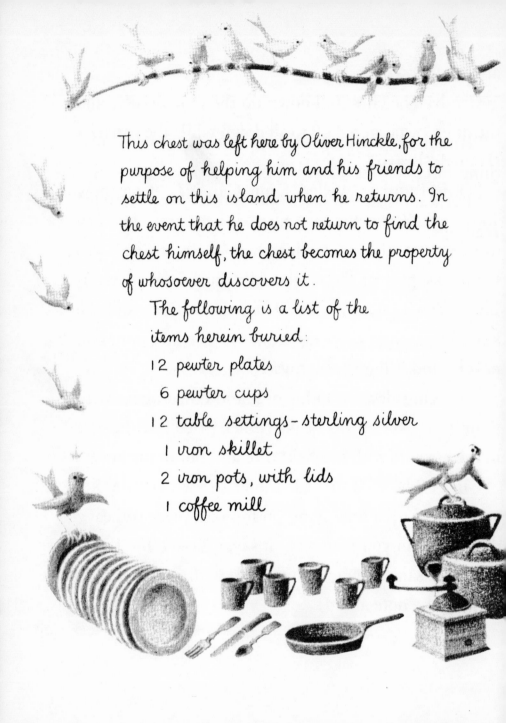

This chest was left here by Oliver Hinckle, for the purpose of helping him and his friends to settle on this island when he returns. In the event that he does not return to find the chest himself, the chest becomes the property of whosoever discovers it.

The following is a list of the items herein buried:

12 pewter plates
6 pewter cups
12 table settings - sterling silver
1 iron skillet
2 iron pots, with lids
1 coffee mill

"Rubbish!" interrupted the King. "Isn't there anything but cooking utensils?"

"Let me finish the list," said Elmer. He continued reading:

> 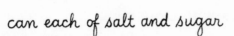 can each of salt and sugar
> 1 axe
> 1 tinder box
> 5 bags seed, including squash, corn, cabbage, wheat and millet
> 1 gold watch and chain, belonging to my wife Sarah
> 1 sterling silver harmonica
> 6 bags of gold pieces

"Gold! I knew it! Just think of it, Queen. Six bags of gold!" trilled the King.

"What will you do with them, King dear?" asked the Queen.

"I won't do anything with them. I'll just have them and be rich."

"Shall I unpack now?" asked Elmer, who was anxious to see the sterling silver harmonica.

"By all means," ordered King Can XI, strutting back and forth in front of the twittering canaries.

Elmer unpacked everything, and at last came to the sterling silver harmonica. He blew on it gently, and the sound was so sweet that all the canaries stopped chattering and listened. The King listened, too, with tears in his eyes. When Elmer had finished playing "The Bear Went Over the Mountain" the King flew up to a branch of the pine and said solemnly, "Elmer, on behalf of the Queen and myself, and all the other Feather Islanders, I want to thank you and your

dragon friend for digging up this treasure and thereby ridding us of the plague of curiosity. I now present you with that silver harmonica, which you play so beautifully, and three of the six bags of gold. And to this brave dragon I present the gold watch and chain. Elmer, fasten it around his neck."

Elmer hooked the chain around the dragon's neck, arranging the watch at his throat. "How's that?" asked Elmer.

"I can't see it, but it feels just fine," said the proud baby dragon.

The birds all clapped their wings and then the

dragon, who really didn't care for speeches, remarked, "Looking at those pots and plates makes me hungry. Let's celebrate and eat something!"

"Goodness!" said the Queen. "I don't believe we've ever had a celebration before. What shall we eat?"

"Tangerines!" said Elmer. "I bet you've never tasted one."

Elmer peeled twelve of the thirty-one tangerines he had left in his knapsack, and put one on each of the twelve pewter plates. Then he hurried off to pick a good mess of skunk cabbages and ostrich ferns for the dragon. When he came back everyone crowded around to feast. Elmer sat beside the dragon and ate nine tangerines all by himself. Then he played "Turkey in the Straw" on the sterling silver harmonica while the King did a jig on a pewter plate. Soon everybody joined in the dancing, and they danced themselves to sleep, all over the pine needles under the great tall tree.

Chapter Nine

FAREWELL

"I think I ought to be getting home," said Elmer the next morning as he ate the last ten tangerines. "How do you feel, Dragon?"

"Fine! Why, I could fly to the moon and back."

"Good," said Elmer, "because I think today is my father's birthday." He looked at the plates and the pots and the cups and the silverware and the bags of seed spread all over the pine needles and asked, "King, what shall we do with your part of the treasure?"

"Dear, dear," said the King. "Well, we can plant the seeds, but I guess we ought to put the rest back in the chest. But my gold! I must have my gold!"

"I insist upon at least one silver spoon," cheeped the Queen.

"Then I'll save out the seeds and a spoon and three pieces of gold," suggested Elmer, who was anxious to be off.

"Better make it five pieces of gold," said the King. "I really ought to give one to Flute."

Elmer packed the chest and gave the key back to the King. "Shall we bury it again?" he asked.

"I suppose so," said the King with tears in his eyes. "I hate to think of it way down there, but at least it will be safe from robbers. But never mind about putting back the dirt. We can do that ourselves."

So the dragon carefully lowered the chest into the hole while Elmer put away the shovel. Then Elmer packed his knapsack with the three bags of gold and the sterling silver harmonica, carefully wrapping the harmonica in the burlap bag left over from the rescue.

"Good-by, everybody, and thanks for a wonderful visit," he shouted to all the canaries. "You can count on me. I'll never tell your secret to a soul."

"Good-by, Elmer, and thanks again," said the King, who was already busy giving orders to the other canaries about filling up the hole.

Flute rode on Elmer's shoulder as he and the dragon walked back to the cliff. "Good-by, Elmer. Please give my best to your mother. She really was awfully good to me, you know."

"I will, Flute, and good-by," said Elmer, wondering if he didn't have some little thing to give Flute. He looked once more in his knapsack and found that he still had three sticks of chewing gum and half a package of rubber bands. "I don't suppose you'd like to have these?" he asked.

"I'd love them," said Flute. "I'll keep them with my gold piece, and I'll be even richer than the King because I'll keep my treasure where I can see it every day."

Flute told Elmer and the dragon the best way to fly to Nevergreen City, and then Elmer hopped aboard, waving farewell to Flute and Feather Island.

Chapter Ten

ELMER FLIES HOME

They flew and flew, the dragon trying hard not to look at, or think about, the wet, wet ocean. Elmer sat watching their shadow rippling over the waves beneath them, feeling washed by the cool morning breeze. The dragon was strong and well rested, being nicely stuffed with skunk cabbages and ostrich ferns, and they hadn't stopped once when he shouted towards evening, "I think I see land ahead!"

"So do I, and I think it's the coast of Popsicornia," yelled Elmer. "Yes, I'm sure it is. There's Firefly Lighthouse. It won't be long now. It's just a few miles up the coast from here."

"Where shall I land when we get there?" asked the

dragon. "Now that I'm free I should hate to be put in a zoo or a circus or something."

"Well, it'll be dark soon. I think you could land on a wharf without attracting attention. Of course, we'll have to be quiet."

They flew up the coast, passing the lighthouse and the Village of Fruitoria and the Town of Custard, and finally came to the outskirts of Nevergreen City.

"There it is!" cried Elmer. "See, that dark patch is Evergreen Park. I live just across the street. Could you land on that long wharf just ahead?"

"I think so," said the dragon, "but I do hope nobody sees me." He circled lower and lower and landed gently on the end of the wharf. Elmer slid off and whispered, "Gosh, it was fun knowing you. I'm going to miss you and flying and everything, and thanks so much for bringing me home."

"It was fun, wasn't it," sniffled the dragon, "and I'll never forget how you came all the way to Wild Island just to rescue me. By the way, Elmer, I really think you ought to have this beautiful gold watch and chain. I can't see it on me, and anyway, I don't even know how to tell time."

"Are you sure? I could give it to my mother. But haven't I got something you'd like to trade it for?"

"Well, as a matter of fact, I was wondering if you still had some of those delicious pink lollipops."

"I have four left over," said Elmer, getting them out and taking off the wrappers. "Would you like all four at once?"

"Yes," said the dragon.

They stood there quietly in the dark, the dragon sucking four pink lollipops, and Elmer whispered, "Where will you go from here?"

"I'll go to find my family in the great high mountains of Blueland," said the dragon, thinking of his six sisters and seven brothers and his gigantic mother and father.

"I'd like to go there too, someday," said Elmer.

"Well, maybe you will, but listen—I hear voices."
"Men coming down the wharf! Quick, you'd better
hurry! Good-by, dear Dragon."

The dragon flew up into the darkness just as two watchmen thumped by to make their rounds. Elmer hid behind a crate and heard one say, "Funny, I was sure I heard voices, and I know I heard something big flying just over our heads."

"Look! Four lollipop wrappers!" said the other watchman, who had been searching the wharf with a lantern.

"Hmm," said the first watchman, and then they walked back down the wharf. Elmer followed them at a distance, and while they were telling another watchman about the lollipop wrappers he ran as fast as he could, through the streets, through Evergreen Park,

all the way home. He leaped up the porch steps three at a time yelling, "Mother, Daddy, I'm home! Happy Birthday!"

Mr. and Mrs. Elevator rushed to the door and threw their arms around Elmer. "Oh, Elmer, how glad we are to see you! You don't know how worried we've been these past two weeks. Where on earth did you go?"

"I had an important job to do," said Elmer, staring at the living-room sofa. "Why, there's my friend the old alley cat!"

"Yes," said Mrs. Elevator. "As much as I've always hated cats, I just didn't have the heart to turn her out. She came to the door the day after you left, and I kept thinking, 'Elmer loved this cat. I really ought to take good care of her.' And do you know, I've grown awfully fond of her in just two weeks."

Elmer rushed over to the cat and whispered, "I rescued the dragon and he just flew me home. He was right where you told me he'd be."

"You did what?" asked Mr. Elevator.

"Oh, nothing," said Elmer. "By the way, here's your birthday present." Elmer gave his father the three bags of gold and played "Happy Birthday" on the sterling silver harmonica. "And here's a beautiful gold watch and chain for you, Mother."

"But where did you ever get these things?" gasped Mr. and Mrs. Elevator.

"That's a secret I can never tell," said Elmer, rummaging in the icebox for something to eat.

THE END